TATERTOWN'S
TALENT SHOW

Springbrook Books

Tatertown's Talent Show

Springbrook Books
Newberg, Oregon
www.springbrookbooks.com

ISBN 978-1-594980-45-9

Thanks to all my family and friends for their support in this project. Special thanks to my wonderful husband, Larry, for his love and encouragement, and to my fabulous sister, Judi Weigandt, for illustrating this book for me.

I would also like to acknowledge and thank my friend, Ruthie Mantinko-Wald, for her guidance and assistance in getting this book published.

TATERTOWN'S TALENT SHOW

GOLDEN SPUD

written by Janice Lathrop
illustrated by Judi Weigandt

Tatertown's Talent Show is finally here.
Potatoes come from far and near.

All are hoping to win the big prize,
excitement and joy showing in their eyes.

Tryouts are scheduled for two o'clock.
Potatoes line up around the block.

The potatoes waiting for tryout time
are shocked to see an onion in line.

"This is Tatertown. Doesn't she know?
Only potatoes are allowed in this show!"

"What nerve she has," they whispered one to another.
"She can't try out. Why even bother?"

"She has no chance," they continued to say.
"Someone should tell her to just go away."

But waiting backstage, they quickly learned
Un Yun is kind. She should have a turn.

They hoped she might be allowed to audition
even though it was against the tradition.

In charge of auditions was Mayor Spud Baker.
He would select the contestants as the
show's common-tater.

Up first was Julienne; he is a French friar.
Playing the violin was his heart's desire.

He played with such love that his violin sang,
The mayor was moved; twas a beautiful thing.

"You're good!" said Spud Baker. "You're in the show.
Now we wait for the rest to go."

Yukon Goldie walked through the door,
sat at the piano, and played a score.

She was so good that Spud wanted to hear more.

"Thumbs up," said Spud Baker. "Yes for her too.
Now let's see what the others can do."

Big Red was up next. He stepped out of the wings, walked to the microphone, and started to sing.

His voice was so pure, so rich, and so mellow. Spud knew the show just needed this fellow.

"Bravo!" said Spud. "You've passed the test. Please go backstage, and wait with the rest."

Next up, the Tater Tots spotted their chance.
The tap dancing trio proved they could dance!

They tapped 'round the stage with such sharp precision.
Spud Baker just smiled. It was an easy decision.

"OK," said Spud. "Now who's the next act?"
Out strode The Mashers, a rock band in fact.

They played with spirit. Spud was impressed.
"Excellent!" he shouted. "You're in the contest."

The next to last act was called The Hash Browns.
It was a group of three, hilarious clowns.

Spud laughed at their antics. He giggled and roared.
"You're in," he howled, and he laughed even more!

The final audition was quite a surprise.
Spud Baker's amazement he couldn't disguise.

Un Yun took the stage all set to perform.
Spud tried to stop her: "This is out of the norm!"

"You're an onion," Spud said. "You can't try out.
This show's for potatoes. That's what it's about."

The potatoes backstage heard all the fuss.
"Let her try out," they said. "It's OK with us."

Un Yun juggled five rings high in the air.
She moved 'round the stage with hardly a care.

The potatoes all watched from behind the curtain.
This onion was good. That was for certain!

She tossed to the left and danced to the right.
She caught every ring, to Spud Baker's delight.

"OK," he said,
"You're on tonight."

Not all who tried out got in the show.
Some were a yes, but some were a no.

Spud was delighted with those who were yes.
He knew this year's show would be one of the best.

The talent show started promptly at eight.
All the potatoes backstage couldn't wait.

Four judges were seated, all in their places.
A look of excitement on each of their faces.

The town hall was large with every seat filled.
When the curtain rose, the spec-taters stilled.

Each act was announced, and they went one by one.
The talent was good; the show was such fun.

But the show wasn't over. There was one act to go.
Un Yun was up last. Would she steal the show?

The spec-taters gasped when Un Yun appeared.
Some were rude. Some even jeered.

"What's she doing here?" they yelled in outrage.
"Only potatoes are allowed up on stage!"

Some of the taters were boiling mad.
Un Yun stood on stage, quiet and sad.

Spud silenced them all, "I said she could go.
Now please sit back down, and enjoy the show."

Un looked at the crowd, wiped a tear from her eye,
then said to herself, "Onions always try."

"I'll pull it together
and throw those rings high."

The five rings she juggled
were hardly a chore.

She danced 'round the stage.
Then she picked up five more!

The taters were stunned
by what she could do.

Ten rings in the air,
and Un Yun could dance, too!

Her performance was perfect
without any flaws.

The spec-taters roared
with thunderous applause.

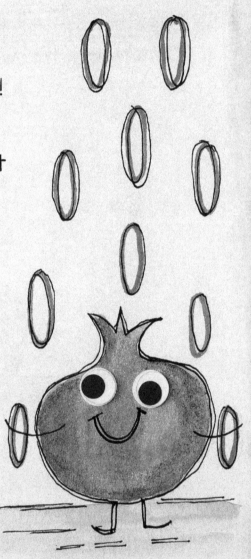

The contest was over, and to no one's surprise,
it was Un Yun
who won the big prize.

She accepted the trophy
with glee and elation.
The audience gave her a standing ovation!

Tatertown realized that very night,
excluding others just isn't right.

The decision was made that all future shows
would welcome all veggies, not just potatoes!

THE END

Hope you can make it to the next
Tatertown Talent Show!

CPSIA information can be obtained
at www.ICGtesting.com
Printed in the USA
LVHW06s1140070518
576114LV00002B/20/P